For my daughter, Elizabeth, who first rode this elephant home; my son, Spencer, who welcomed him; and my wife, Lily, who lovingly nurtures my elephantine dreams—L.B.

To my parents—A.J.

Published by Schwartz & Wade Books ~ an imprint of Random House Children's Books ~ a division of Random House, Inc. ~ New York ~ Text copyright © 2008 by Lou Berger Illustrations copyright © 2008 by Ana Juan ~ All rights reserved. ~ Schwartz & Wade Books and colophon are trademarks of Random House, Inc. Visit us on the Web! www.randomhouse.com/kids ~ Educators and librarians, for a variety of teaching tools, visit us at www.randomhouse.com/teachers

Library of Congress Cataloging-in-Publication Data ~ Berger, Lou. ~ The elephant wish / Lou Berger ; illustrated by Ana Juan. — 1st ed. ~ p. cm. ~ Summary: Soon after wishing that an elephant will come and take her away from her too-busy parents, Eliza's fondest desire comes true but her journey is observed by ninety-seven-year-old Adelle, who once made the same wish. ~ ISBN 978-0-375-83962-7 (trade) ISBN 978-0-375-93962-4 (lib. bdg.)
[1. Wishes—Fiction. 2. Elephants—Fiction. 3. Family life—Fiction.]
I. Juan, Ana, ill. II. Title. ~ PZ7.B45213Ele 2008 ~ [Fic]—dc22 ~ 2007034329

The text of this book is set in EideticNeo. ~ The illustrations are rendered in acrylic colors and crayon.
PRINTED IN CHINA
1 3 5 7 9 10 8 6 4 2
First Edition

THE ELEPHANT WISH

BY LOU BERGER

ILLUSTRATED BY ANA JUAN

schwartz & wade books · new york

C ousin Floyd appeared for the first time two days, six hours, thirty-seven minutes, and nine seconds from the moment Eliza Prattlebottom blew out eight candles and wished her birthday wish.

Eliza's father thought Eliza had wished he would take off his eye patch and finally wear the blue glass eye that he kept in a cuff link box next to his bed.

Eliza's mother thought Eliza had wished she would give up her role as Third Witch in the Metropolitan Opera's new production of Verdi's *Macbeth.*

They were both wrong.

This was Eliza Prattlebottom's wish: *Oh, I wish that an elephant would come and take me away!*

You probably think that a large elephant in a black floppy hat, trumpeting down Bunthmather Street, would be noticed. He was.

Adelle, who was ninety-seven years old, with perfect posture and wavy white hair that you wanted to scoop like snow, saw him while she was pulling her two-hundred-year-old bulldog, Potato, in a red wagon.

A moment later . . .

. . . it was as if she hadn't seen him at all.

And at 200 Bunthmather Street, a wish came true. Eliza was lying in bed, looking at the colors that appeared behind her eyelids whenever she closed them tightly. Upstairs, her mother was singing like a Witch. Suddenly, Eliza's skin felt excited. A warm breeze blew through her room, ruffling her hair.

Eliza knew what was happening!
She raced to the front door, opened
it, and saw a wrinkly gray mass with
a squinty bright eye.

A nozzled trunk lifted her, and
with her heart thumping in her chest,
she hopped onto the back of Cousin
Floyd.

Floyd took off at four times the
speed of wind, and the street became
a whoosh of color.

There are three rules when riding an elephant:

1. Don't fall off.

2. If you fall off, fall onto something soft.

3. *There is nothing soft enough, so don't fall off.*

Eliza did *not* fall off, even when Floyd kicked
up the speed to Wind Five.

Her father, sitting at a long table where men and women talked of percentages, doodled pictures of Eliza on a yellow legal pad.

Her mother, the Witch in the middle, sang beautifully but seemed sadder than the witches to her right and left.

At night, they dreamed of Eliza. Eliza laughing, Eliza angry, Eliza dancing, Eliza stubborn—the night was filled with Elizas.

Sometimes her father would awaken, look at his glass eye lit by the moon, and in the blueness of the eye, see Eliza walking with a family of elephants. One hand would be holding the tail of the elephant in front, the other holding the trunk of the elephant behind. The elephant in front would be wearing a big floppy hat.

Adele could not sleep at all these days. Often she'd sit up and remember a time long ago when she was a little girl named Addie who had wished for an elephant, and how an elephant had come to her farm, and she'd jumped from a haystack onto its back. She'd remember a journey across sidewalks and stars, and she'd remember the lake and the mud and her elephant family dancing in a circle.

One night, she sat for hours
remembering. And then, near dawn,
she put Potato in his red wagon and
pulled him around the corner.

Adelle had decided to find Cousin Floyd. She needed to be with him once again.

Now, you might think that a ninety-seven-year-old woman pulling a wagon with a two-hundred-year-old dog in it would move very slowly. But Adelle was moving at the speed of memory.

She remembered playing with her brothers and sisters, and touching the stubble on her grandpa's face. She drove a tractor again, sitting on her father's lap, and fell asleep on the old green picnic table while her mother washed her hair and hummed.

She traveled all the places she'd ever been—
along dirt roads and highways, over mountains,
across oceans, and under stars . . .

. . . until the world began to look jungly and
the night became hot and she could hear
the calls of hidden creatures.

In a clearing, she saw a family of elephants walking slowly in a circle, lit by the same moon as on Bunthmather Street.

Eliza was there, too.

Adelle recognized the elephant in the black floppy hat, and her eyes lit up with joy. "Cousin Floyd!" she cried.

The elephants continued their slow, steady circle-walk.

"It's me, Cousin Floyd! Addie!"

The large elephant
stopped and gave forth a
mighty trumpeting blast.
Slowly he stomped toward the
ninety-seven-year-old woman
with perfect posture.

Tilting his head, he gazed at her out of one ancient squinty eye. Then he stooped down as if bowing and touched Adelle's hair with his trunk.

"Yes, it's me," she said. "I've come back."

After a long time, and with a great effort, Adelle called out, "Eliza, come here!"
Eliza did not move.

"Eliza Prattlebottom of Two Hundred Bunthmather Street—come to me now!"

Eliza took a small step forward.

Adelle spoke to Cousin Floyd. "Take her home."

"No! No! I want to stay!" Eliza protested. And then, proud—"I'm an elephant!" And she threw back her head and trumpeted.

Cousin Floyd threw back his head, too, and trumpeted.

And Potato, excited, howled in his wagon.

As the trumpeting echoed through the jungle, Adelle said again, "Take her home."

"NO!" shouted Eliza.

If a large elephant wearing a black floppy hat can look sad, then Cousin Floyd looked sad. His look also said, "One of you must go. I can't hold two wishers at the same time."

Adelle spoke with the force of ninety-seven years. "Oh, Eliza, you have days and months and years. You have friends you haven't met and a life that you must not wish away. Go home."

But the old woman's words only made Eliza fiercer and more stubborn.

"NO!"

The jungle became very still.

Now old Adelle seemed to become a little girl again. And it was this little girl from long ago who pleaded with Eliza. "Oh, don't make me go back, I need to stay. *Please?*"

"But why did you leave the first time?" Eliza asked.

"Grandpa came. Riding his tractor. He took me home. And I wished and I wished, but Cousin Floyd never came again, and I lived my life and was happy, and I forgot for a while. But now I'm here, and I've waited so long, and I *can't* go away again."

It was the child that Eliza could not say no to. She had to grant the little girl's wish.

And in that moment, Cousin Floyd lifted Eliza Prattlebottom onto his back, and together they ran through the jungle at the speed of Wind Five.

Bunthmather St.

Tokyo

The Jungle

Eliza did not fall off until they turned the corner of Bunthmather Street and Cousin Floyd placed her at her own front door.

With the elephant ride still vibrating through her body, Eliza raised a hand to wave goodbye.

And Cousin Floyd raised his trunk and gave one final trumpeting blast.

When Eliza entered her house, everything looked smaller and different, as if she was a stranger visiting. Her parents swooped upon her, and though they didn't understand where their girl had been, they promised to spend more time with her. But for now their lives were still busy.

Her mother was singing
the Second Wicked Stepsister
in Rossini's *Cinderella.*

Her father had been
promoted to the head of
the long table, where the
color of his eye patch now
always matched his tie.

Sixty-three days, five
hours, and twenty-seven minutes
later, Eliza found a friend who
made her laugh like no one else,
and together they created a
secret language.

Six years, five months, nine days, and sixteen minutes from the time she returned home, she met a boy who sang to her, only to her.

And in her long life she had many adventures and did many things.

But sometimes at night, lying in bed, the
trees outside her window making leafy shadows
on the moonlit wall, she remembered walking
with the elephants—trunk to tail, tail to trunk,
the biggest elephant wearing a black floppy hat.

And she saw old Adelle, perfect
posture, beautiful white hair,
holding the tail of the elephant
in front of her, while her other hand
still clutched the handle of
the red wagon, as she pulled
Potato behind her.